Laws That Changed History

Key LABOR LAWS

Cavendish Square
New York

Alex Acks

Published in 2020 by Cavendish Square Publishing, LLC

243 5th Avenue, Suite 136, New York, NY 10016

First Edition

Website: cavendishsq.com

Cataloging-in-Publication Data

Names: Acks, Alex.
Title: Key labor laws / Alex Acks.
Description: New York : Cavendish Square Publishing, 2020. | Series: Laws that changed history | Includes glossary and index.
Identifiers: ISBN 9781502655295 (pbk.) | ISBN 9781502655301 (library bound) | ISBN 9781502655318 (ebook)
Subjects: LCSH: Labor laws and legislation--United States--History--Juvenile literature. | Labor--United States--History--Juvenile literature.
Classification: LCC KF3319.A72 2020 | DDC 344.7301--dc23

Printed in China

Photo Credits: Cover, p. 1 sirtravelalot/Shutterstock.com; pp. 4-5 Mark Wilson/Getty Images; p. 8 Robert W. Kelley/The LIFE Picture Collection/Getty Images; pp. 9, 16 Copyright © North Wind Picture Archives; pp. 10-11, 21, 26-27, 28, 30-31, 40-41, 44-45 Bettmann/Getty Images; pp. 18, 47 Pacific Press/LightRocket/Getty Images; pp. 23, 51 © AP Images; p. 33 Rex Hardy Jr./The LIFE Picture Collection/Getty Images; p. 36 Fred Stein Archive/Archive Photos/Getty Images; pp. 38-39 Universal History Archive/Universal Images Group/Getty Images; p. 43 Hulton Archive/Archive Photos/Getty Images; pp. 48-49 Fotosearch/Archive Photos/Getty Images; pp. 54-55 a katz/Shutterstock.com; p. 57 Rachael Warriner/Shutterstock.com; p. 58 Saul Loeb/AFP/Getty Images; p. 60 Alex Wong/Getty Images; cover, back cover, and interior pages capitol dome graphic Alexkava/Shutterstock.com.

CONTENTS

Introduction

It started with an anonymous note in a work mailbox in 1998. Lilly Ledbetter, a manager at Goodyear Tire and Rubber, picked up the innocuous piece of paper and was devastated by what she read.[1] The note told her the salaries of a few of her male colleagues. After nineteen years as the only woman in a job title she shared with fifteen men, she was making drastically less than her male colleagues, who were being paid 24 to 40 percent more than her for doing the same work.[2]

At Goodyear, performance evaluations determined raises for managers. Ledbetter had received several poor evaluations early on, which she felt were the result of gender discrimination rather than a true reflection of her performance.[3] The early bad evaluations kept her pay low compared to her male coworkers, since raises were always a percentage of current salary.

In July of 1998, Ledbetter filed formal charges with the Equal Employment Opportunity Commission (EEOC).

The first law President Barack Obama signed was the Lilly Ledbetter Fair Pay Act of 2009.

Founded in 1965, the EEOC enforces civil rights laws against discrimination related to race, national origin, religion, sex, age, disability, and other categories.[4] In 1999, after she retired early, Ledbetter sued Goodyear for gender-based pay discrimination under Title VII of the Civil Rights Act and the Equal Pay Act.[5]

Initially, Ledbetter was victorious. A district court allowed the claim under the Civil Rights Act to go to trial. The jury tried to award her more than $3.5 million, which the judge reduced to $360,000 due to limits put in place by Title VII.[6] However, Goodyear appealed, citing that under Title VII, complaints with the EEOC have to be lodged no more than 180 days "after the alleged unlawful employment practice occurred." The Supreme Court ultimately agreed, voting 5–4. Ledbetter was eighteen years too late filing her complaint, even though with every paycheck the discrimination she had faced chipped away at her wages.[7]

Ruth Bader Ginsburg, the only female justice on the Supreme Court at the time, read her dissent from the bench, a rare move that showed how strenuously she disagreed with the majority.[8] Justice Ginsburg said, "The Court does not comprehend or is indifferent to the insidious way in which women can be victims of pay discrimination."[9]

Lilly Ledbetter walked away with nothing, but she kept fighting against pay discrimination. On January 29, 2009, the Lilly Ledbetter Fair Pay Act of 2009 became the first law that President Barack Obama signed. The act reset the 180-day clock at each paycheck that showed discriminatory effect.[10]

The Pew Research Center showed that in 2015, black and Hispanic men as well as women of all races earned significantly less than white men.[11] As of 2017, women as a group still generally earned 89 cents to every dollar a man earned.[12] Lilly Ledbetter's law is only one recent battle waged on a front that stretches back to the Industrial Revolution in America.

CHAPTER 1

Labor vs. Monopolies

As long as there have been working people, they've been at odds with those who pay them. With the massive shift from subsistence farming to factory work that the Industrial Revolution caused starting around 1790, this divide became even more noticeable.

In America, the new "working class" was largely made up of immigrants and people from rural areas who had moved to the cities. Wealth flowed into the hands of the people who owned the factories, while wages for the workers remained low.[1] Factory owners sought to employ women and children because they could be paid less due to their age or sex. Whole families had to work long hours because wages were kept so low. Working conditions were dangerous or unsanitary; it cost more money for things to be safe and clean. Workers sometimes didn't have enough money for food and lived in slums or in villages owned by the same people who owned the factory.[2] Workers were disposable because there was always someone else next in line who was desperate for any job.

Martin Luther King Jr. (*center*) marched for civil rights, which included the right to a good job at a fair wage

Workers began to organize to fight for better conditions; while one person walking off the job could be ignored, every worker in a factory leaving would stop production in its tracks. In 1834, the owners of the textile mills in Lowell, Massachusetts, decided that they were paying the girls who tended the machines too much and cut their wages. The girls, furious, "turned out," meaning they walked out of work, and they went to other nearby factories to recruit more women for their protest. Their action was what we'd call a "strike" today.

This first strike was unsuccessful; the mill girls were forced to return to work, and the bosses took petty revenge on their families, such as taking away their rooms at boarding houses. The mill girls turned out again in 1836 after another round of wage cuts and were similarly unsuccessful. In the 1840s, they changed tactics, organizing the Lowell Female Labor Reform Association (LFLRA), with chapters spreading through Massachusetts and nearby New Hampshire. They ran petition drives and distributed pamphlets depicting the terrible conditions of the factory, pushing to have their workdays legally reduced to a maximum of ten hours.[3] In response, New Hampshire made the ten-hour workday the law in 1847, but the law said employees could voluntarily choose to work longer.[4] In practice, this meant employees often had to work late anyway or risk being fired in favor of another employee who would.

The LFLRA was the first labor union for women in the United States and marked the beginning of an era of organized

The Lowell Female Labor Reform Association was established by women working at textile mills. It was the first union for working women.

action by working-class people. The Brotherhood of Locomotive Engineers and Trainmen was founded in 1863, a little less than thirty years after the Lowell mill girls first turned out. Soon, larger unions began to span the United States.

After the Thirteenth Amendment

In the Emancipation Proclamation, Abraham Lincoln declared on January 1, 1863, that all enslaved people in the Confederate states (but not those in the Union states) were free. The Thirteenth Amendment followed a little less than three years later, making slavery illegal except as punishment for a crime.[5] The greatest immediate effect of these documents was to add nearly 4 million people who had once been enslaved to the free workforce.[6] When the Thirteenth Amendment was being debated in Congress, the idea that freedom is necessary for the well-being of laborers was prominent. Senator Henry Wilson explained: "We have advocated the rights of the black man because the black man was the most oppressed type of the toiling men of this country … The same influences that go to keep down and crush down the rights of the poor black man bear down and oppress the poor white laboring man."[7]

The time after the American Civil War was one of social upheaval. The first movement for female suffrage was launched, partly powered by working women. Workers in the North fought to better their conditions with strikes and other direct action, some of which was violent. Across America, unions proliferated, aided in the South by Reconstruction governments that recognized labor's right to organize.[8] Black workers exercised their new ability

The Brotherhood of Sleeping Car Porters was the first union led by black men to be admitted into the American Federation of Labor.

for collective action; for instance, in 1881, a union of black women laundresses in Atlanta called the Washing Society went on strike to demand higher pay. They inspired other domestic workers to do the same.[9]

The working class was not a united entity, however. Prior to the Civil War, free black workers were often excluded from the unions of white workers. After the war, with union membership growing rapidly, black workers were still excluded. They founded their own unions, such as the Brotherhood of Sleeping Car Porters. White unions sometimes directly attacked black workers, whom they viewed to be competition rather than compatriots. In 1909, Brotherhood of Locomotive Firemen and Enginemen workers walked out of their jobs at the Georgia Railroad because they wanted black workers, who already had lower wages, to be replaced with white union workers.[10]

Organizations such as the National Labor Union tried to unite unions of diverse race and gender to fight for the same cause. However, the NLU excluded Chinese immigrant workers at its founding. This frustrating division along racial lines often had labor fighting against itself rather than the actual source of workers' misery.

Driven by advances in railroad technology, industry and agriculture experienced massive booms. Companies grew large and built themselves into monopolies, headed by ruthless "robber barons" who had no problem with using political favors and hired muscle to crush labor revolts and business competition alike. The massive wealth these tycoons amassed, in contrast to the poverty their workers lived in gave this period, from about 1870 to 1900, its name: the Gilded Age, because "gilded" means covered in gold.

By this time, the wealth gap between the richest and poorest had become impossible to ignore; the richest 1 percent in America had more money than the poorest 50 percent. Poor workers scavenged for firewood when coal became too expensive to buy, while wealthy business owners lived in excessive luxury; while many workers went hungry, the rich spent thousands of dollars on food and clothing. Desperate workers who felt they had nothing to lose went on strike; company guards, police, or National Guardsmen clashed with the strikers, often violently. In "American Labor Violence: Its Causes, Character, and Outcome," part of a broader 1969 government study on the history of violence in America, the authors noted, "The United States has had the bloodiest and most violent labor history of any industrial nation in the world."[11]

The Arbitration Act of 1888

In 1873, a financial crisis triggered an economic depression in the United States and Europe that lasted four years later. In July of 1877, the Baltimore & Ohio (B&O) Railroad announced a second round of wage cuts for work that already had low wages.

Workers in Martinsburg, West Virginia, uncoupled locomotives and refused to allow any trains through the station. Governor Henry M. Mathews first sent militia soldiers to try to break up the strike, then requested federal troops, something that wasn't uncommon at that time. The federal troops got the trains running again, but by then the strike had spread up the line and to other railroads. National Guard units were sent to Pittsburgh and charged striking workers there, which started a riot. Forty people died over two days, prompting a general strike in the city. Strikes continued to spread throughout July until they were eventually broken by National Guard units in a multitude of cities. By the time the strike had ended, more than 100,000 workers had been involved, and around 100 had been killed.[12]

While the Great Railroad Strike of 1877 accomplished very little for workers because the federal government was willing to send troops to defend the interests of business, it showed just how disruptive railroad strikes could be. There were also many smaller railroad strikes throughout the 1870s and 1880s.

The Arbitration Act of 1888 was a first step by the federal government to imagine a kind of intervention in these labor disputes that didn't involve sending National Guardsmen into the fray. It established arbitration boards that would mediate in labor disputes between companies and unions. This was meant to reduce the number of strikes. The federal government now had an interest in ending strikes without violence and offered unions a seat at the table, instead of reserving federal intervention only for company owners.[13]

Lucy Parsons: "More Dangerous Than a Thousand Rioters"

Born in 1853 to parents of Native American, black, and Mexican ancestry, Lucy Parsons probably began her life enslaved. When she was twenty, she moved to Chicago with her husband Albert, a former Confederate soldier who became an anarchist newspaper editor.

Lucy, a socialist and anarchist, organized workers in Chicago and led thousands on strikes to protest poverty and abusive working conditions. Her husband was one of the four anarchists hanged after the Haymarket Riot of 1886; after his death, Lucy continued to lead protests and give lectures, which the police, who said she was "more dangerous than a thousand rioters," often tried to shut down before she could even reach the podium. In 1905, she helped found the Industrial Workers of the World (IWW), a radical union that sought to unite workers across all trades and industries.[14]

The act depended on voluntary arbitration, meaning both parties had to agree to bargain with each other, but this didn't always happen. In June–July 1894, the Pullman Palace Car Company cut the wages of its workers (who already worked sixteen-hour days) by 25 percent but didn't reduce any rents or fees in the company-owned town of Pullman. Pullman workers went on strike, and workers in the American Railway Union joined in a sympathetic boycott, refusing to handle any trains that had Pullman cars in them. By June 30, 125,000 Pullman and ARU workers had walked off the job. The federal government responded with a court injunction, and President Grover Cleveland sent in troops soon after. Violent protests spiraled out of control, culminating in guardsmen killing two people during a riot. When the strike ended, Pullman hired workers back after forcing them to sign a pledge that they would not join a union—and President Cleveland attempted to reconcile with workers by declaring Labor Day a national holiday.[15]

The Sherman Antitrust Act of 1890

By 1890, the government had become concerned by the concentration of power in industrial monopolies, such as Standard Oil. The Sherman Antitrust Act aimed to break up "combinations" that restrained trade between the states, which included businesses that prevented competition.

Generally, this was a positive move for workers. Economically, labor is subject to supply and demand just like goods. When there is competition for labor by different companies, workers have more power. They can choose to seek employment elsewhere if they don't like their wages or conditions. When there are monopolies, workers have nowhere else to go and are forced to accept the monopoly's terms.

Right after its passage, the Sherman Act was only rarely used against monopolies—but it was used against unions,

During the Pullman Strike in 1894, guardsmen fired on workers who wanted union recognition, better wages, and reduced rents.

including during the Pullman Strike. In a court case called *Loewe v. Lawlor*, the Supreme Court decided that a solidarity strike by the United Hatters of North America was illegal.[16] This was not in line with the intentions of Congress, and the Clayton Antitrust Act of 1914 later declared that unions were not conspiracies in violation of antitrust laws. However, the Clayton Act still didn't give unions immunity from prosecution for actions such as solidarity strikes.[17]

CHAPTER 2

The Lochner Era

The Gilded Age ended around 1900. The following "Progressive Era" was marked by massive social activism and reform. Because the Arbitration Act had proven to be weak, it was replaced with the Erdman Act in 1898. This required any labor disputes in the railroad industry to be mediated, and Section 10 of the law said employers couldn't require employees not to form or join a union. However, ten years later, the Supreme Court of the United States decided in a court case called *Adair v. United States* that Section 10 was unconstitutional, so that part was struck down. From that point on, employers had more freedom to make rules that hurt their workers. While courts had ruled against workers in the past, this case was part of an era of extreme hostility by the Supreme Court to any law that infringed on "economic liberty" or "private contract." This became known as the Lochner Era after the case that marked its beginning.[1]

Despite great gains, workers continue to take to the streets to make themselves heard. The 40-hour workweek only began in 1940, not even 100 years ago.

Lochner v. New York

While changes to national laws that affected the conditions of workers were slow to come, some states did attempt to legislate improvements to the lives of workers. One such law was New York's Bakeshop Act of 1895, which regulated health conditions in bakeries. The act also said that workers couldn't work more than ten hours per day or sixty hours per week.

Joseph Lochner owned a bakery in Utica and had been fined twice under the law for "permitting" an employee to work more than sixty hours in a week. He appealed his second fine all the way to the Supreme Court of the United States, claiming that he shouldn't have been fined based on the Fourteenth Amendment, which says, "… nor shall any State deprive any person of life, liberty, or property without due process of law." His argument was not that he was being deprived of those things by the fine—but that the state regulating how many hours the bakers could work deprived *them* of liberty. In effect, the bakers were free people who had a right to work as many hours as they wanted.

Justice Rufus Peckham agreed, saying, "There is no reasonable ground for interfering with the liberty of person or the right of free contract by determining the hours of labor in the occupation of baker. There is no contention that bakers as a class are not equal in intelligence and capacity to men in other trades or manual occupations, or that they are not able to assert their rights and care for themselves without the protecting arm of the state."[2]

Twelve years later, the Supreme Court did uphold a ten-hour workday in the case of *Bunting v. Oregon*. The Oregon law also required overtime wages for up to three hours per day. The difference was that Bunting's case hinged on the law being one that regulated wages instead of work hours, so the court dismissed his argument.[3]

Hammer v. Dagenhart

Driven by determined campaigns against child labor by groups such as the National Child Labor Committee and horrific exposés by journalists, some state governments tried to stop child labor. These laws were often not effective, and factory owners complained that they put them at a competitive disadvantage when some states still allowed child labor. Other states, particularly in the South, resisted any reform.[4] Congress passed the Keating-Owen Child Labor Act in 1916, which prohibited the sale of goods between states that were produced in factories that employed children under fourteen or mines that employed children under sixteen.[5]

The act was immediately challenged by Roland Dagenhart, who worked at a cotton mill in North Carolina with his two sons, who would lose their jobs because of the law. The case went to the Supreme Court, which handed down a 5–4 decision that said this was an abuse of congressional regulatory power because the way the goods were manufactured wasn't actually commerce. Despite the fact that, at the time, the court allowed Congress to regulate "immoral goods" such as gambling machines, the immorality of how a good might have been made didn't count. The court also decided that the attempt to regulate child labor was an unconstitutional intrusion of Congress into powers reserved for the states by the Tenth Amendment, saying, "the act in a two-fold sense is repugnant to the Constitution." Justice Oliver Wendell Holmes, in the dissenting opinion, noted, "if there is any matter upon which civilized countries have agreed—it is the evil of premature and excessive child labor."[6]

Laws banning child labor remained a largely unenforceable matter for the states for the next twenty-three years until *United States v. Darby Lumber Co.*, when the court unanimously decided that Congress could regulate working conditions. The opinion referred back to the dissent of Justice Holmes as "powerful and now classic."[7]

Minimum Wage

Activist organizations of laborers and those sympathetic to their plight thought wages should not fall below the amount needed for the "necessities of life"—that there should be a legal minimum wage. The first successful minimum wage law was passed in New Zealand in 1894. The first minimum wage law in the United States was passed in Massachusetts in

Shown here are young men picketing the New York state capitol, demanding a higher minimum wage from Governor Nelson Rockefeller years after the first debates about this issue were heard.

1912 after a ten-week strike by textile workers in Lawrence. The Massachusetts law isn't what we'd expect today; it only established a state commission that recommended minimum wages for women and children.[8]

As the Great Depression descended in 1929, the need for there to be a minimum wage became even more apparent as desperate workers were forced to compete for less and less money. Twenty-five states had minimum-wage laws by 1938, but the Supreme Court remained hostile to those laws, viewing them as a violation of "freedom to contract" rather than a protection from abuse by employers. In cases such as *Adkins v. Children's Hospital* (1923)[9] and *Morehead v. New York* (1936)[10],

Worker's Compensation Laws

Workers' compensation has a long history, going back to Sumeria in 2050 BCE. Nippur Tablet No. 3191 specifies monetary compensation for specific kinds of on-the-job injuries. In the modern era, workers' compensation laws were started by Chancellor Otto von Bismarck of Prussia. He outlawed the socialists whose activism had been politically inconvenient for him but took up parts of their agenda, such as social insurance, as a calculated political move. He saw to the passage of a workers' accident insurance program in 1884.

The United States paid attention to these developments in Europe and began its own federal reforms, though laws were mostly left to the states. In 1911, Wisconsin became the first state to pass a comprehensive worker's compensation law. Other states followed, with Mississippi being the last in 1948.[11]

the Supreme Court found minimum wage laws unconstitutional as a violation of due process by the states, even as it said that federal regulation of labor was also unconstitutional because that power was reserved to the states.

After *Morehead v. New York*, the Republican Party added a plan to its 1936 platform, which read, "We pledge ourselves to ... support the adoption of State laws to abolish sweatshops and child labor and to protect women and children with respect to maximum hours, minimum wages and working conditions."[12]

The Commission on Industrial Relations

October 1, 1910, seemed like the peak of horror and labor violence in a time wracked by violent strikes. A bomb made from sixteen sticks of dynamite attached to an alarm clock destroyed the Los Angeles Times Building at 1 a.m., killing twenty-one people. The explosion was so powerful that people for blocks around ran in panic, thinking it was an earthquake. Two similar bombs failed to kill their targets that night because they jammed. The McNamara brothers, one of whom was an official of the International Association of Bridge and Structural Iron Workers, were arrested for the crime.

Around that time, union leaders across the country were investigated and arrested for funding bombings of nonunion construction projects.[13] Prompted by the escalating violence, Congress created the Commission on Industrial Relations on

In the early twentieth century, twenty-one people were killed when the Los Angeles Times Building was destroyed with dynamite. It was one of many attacks in the name of organized labor.

August 23, 1912. The commission's responsibilities included investigation into labor conditions as well as unions and how they affected the relationship between employers and employees.

Several major strikes occurred during the three years the commission was active, including the Colorado Fuel and Iron Company Strike, which culminated in the Ludlow Massacre. After armed clashes between miners and company guards, the governor of Colorado called in the National Guard. On April 20, 1914, a fourteen-hour standoff began. The tent city the miners had set up for themselves after being kicked out of their company-owned lodgings when the strike began was pelted with machine gun bullets and then set on fire by the guardsmen. At least eighteen strikers were dead by the end of the day, including two women and eleven children who suffocated in a pit they were hiding in due to the fire.[14] The leader of the Commission on Industrial Relations, Frank P. Walsh, questioned the owner of Colorado Fuel and Iron, John D. Rockefeller Jr., mercilessly for three days.

In the end, the commission published three different reports because the nine members couldn't agree on the results—and little was done legislatively with those reports. The majority report, signed by only five commissioners, advocated the creation of labor boards that could oversee conflicts impartially. The two minority reports were more fiery in their assessment. The minority report authored by attorney Basil Manly stated in its conclusions, "The crux of the question rather is, Have the workers received a fair share of the enormous increase in wealth which has taken place in this country, during the period, as a result largely of their labors? The answer is emphatically, No!"[15]

CHAPTER 3

Labor and the New Deal

During the "Roaring Twenties," union membership in mining, factories, and agriculture fell after a series of terrible defeats by big businesses in the courts. The remaining unions focused on working cooperatively with employers and dropped their more radical demands. While earlier unions had been hotbeds of anarchism and socialism, in the 1920s, the leaders of the largest unions were mostly capitalists who happily expelled radical members. Corruption within union organizations also began to rise.[1]

Arguably, the weakening of organized labor—which resulted in lower wages for the working class across the board—contributed to the Great Depression. While the profits of businesses grew up to 65 percent during the 1920s, wages for workers only went up about 8 percent. If workers wanted access to the goods they were making in factories, such as refrigerators, cars, and clothing, they had to use credit.[2]

As the Great Depression hit, unions lost more members as masses of people became unemployed. Enormous tent cities of

The Great Depression saw record numbers of people out of work. Shown here are men standing in line to register for emergency unemployment relief.

homeless people sprang up. While some companies tried to maintain the wage levels, even the nicest employers were forced to cut wages as the Depression deepened. Strikes began to spread, with nonunion workers banding together in workplaces that had driven out unions in the 1920s. The unemployed began to organize as well to help each other and to protest their desperate circumstances.

The government under President Herbert Hoover took small steps toward helping labor, such as passing the Norris-LaGuardia Act of 1932, which stopped courts from interfering with nonviolent labor disputes and banned "yellow-dog" contracts that prevented workers from joining unions.[3] It was too little, too late; protecting the rights of workers to organize didn't mean much when so many didn't even have a workplace. Things started to change more quickly in 1932 with the election of Franklin D. Roosevelt (FDR) and the introduction of his sweeping array of reform programs known as the New Deal.

The National Industrial Recovery Act of 1933

Soon after the inauguration of FDR, Congress passed the National Industrial Recovery Act (NIRA), which suspended antitrust laws and encouraged the formation of monopolies based on the idea that less competition would

First Lady Eleanor Roosevelt (*center*) rides into a coal mine in 1935 with members of the United Mine Workers and mine officials. Her goal was to better understand the conditions and hazards of the work being done.

help industries recover more quickly. NIRA also banned child labor and set out minimum wages and maximum hours for workers—sweeping reforms that many had desperately fought for in earlier decades.[4] Employers still had the power to hire and fire employees whenever they liked, even though NIRA included the right of workers to organize.

Though it soon became apparent the government wouldn't enforce the pro-labor provisions, unions used NIRA to advertise for new members. The United Mine Workers handed out pamphlets that read, "The President wants you to join a union."

Membership spiked. The United Textile Workers engaged in the biggest strike in American history, with 400,000 workers forcing textile mills across multiple states to stop production as workers called for enforcement of the labor protections of NIRA. They were ultimately unsuccessful; the minimum wages and maximum hours remained largely unenforced.

On May 27, 1935, the Supreme Court found NIRA unconstitutional in the case *Schechter Poultry Corp. v. United States*. While the court's opinion focused mostly on the unconstitutional delegation of Congress's powers to the president, it made sure to note that the federal government still could not regulate wages and hours for workers.[5]

National Labor Relations Act of 1935

The National Labor Relations Act (NLRA) replaced NIRA and was ultimately enforced much more effectively. Unions weren't just recognized; their existence was specifically protected, and employers were legally prohibited from using intimidation tactics, threats, or hiring discrimination. Employers were required to bargain with unions, and workers' votes on union business were kept secret so emloyers couldn't retaliate against specific people. Among its many provisions, the NLRA specifically states, "Nothing in this Act shall be construed so as to interfere with or impede or diminish in any way the right to strike."

The NLRA also established the National Labor Relations Board (NLRB); the job of the board was to enforce the provisions of the NLRA, such as policing unfair labor practices. It was a government entity charged with listening to and investigating the complaints of unions against employers. However, to get enforcement from the board, a union had to agree to abide by all of its union conduct rules, which meant its members could not engage in solidarity strikes.[6]

Businesses were not happy, but unions were generally optimistic as they saw NLRA might actually be enforced. The next year, Roosevelt coasted to reelection on the votes of millions of workers.

The Social Security Act of 1935

The Social Security Act (SSA) is mostly viewed now as a law that helps the elderly and disabled. In 1935, it established what is effectively a national pensions system funded by payroll taxes taken from every worker. The SSA in 1935 also contained provisions that helped workers who were nowhere near retirement. It created an incentive for states to have unemployment insurance programs, which pay benefits to workers who have lost their jobs. These benefits were intended to help them survive until they could find new jobs. The SSA created minimum standards for state unemployment programs and then established a national tax on businesses that would be mostly credited back to them if they were already paying taxes for state unemployment insurance. States that met the minimum standards for unemployment insurance got federal grants to help their programs.

Since the creation of this national unemployment insurance effort, there have been times during economic crises when the federal government has extended unemployment benefits for extra weeks to help those who are out of work.[7]

Fair Labor Standards Act of 1938

In 1937, the attitude of the Supreme Court shifted as one of the conservative justices retired and a frustrated Roosevelt hatched a plan with Congress to try to pack the court with more progressive justices. In the Supreme Court case *West Coast*

In the early 1900s, children were regularly employed in factories and coal mines. In 1938, the Fair Labor Standards Act ended that.

Hotel Co. v. Parrish in 1937, the court upheld minimum wage legislation, overturning its previous position. The Lochner Era and its hostility toward labor was officially ended.[8]

This was a signal for Congress to bring up new labor standards legislation to replace those struck down by the court's NIRA decision. The Fair Labor Standards Act (FLSA) contained everything unions had been striking for and advocates had been campaigning for: an end to child labor, the right to a minimum wage, and overtime pay for anyone working over forty hours. The child labor provision prohibited work for anyone under sixteen in normal conditions and anyone under eighteen in hazardous jobs.[9] While FLSA only covered workers who were employed by companies engaged in interstate commerce, it was still a massive step forward.

The Employment Act of 1946

The New Deal showed that the federal government could take an interest in and regulate the conditions of all workers in the country. The Employment Act of 1946 showed an even bigger shift in the government's view of its responsibilities. The law stated, "The Congress declares that it is the continuing policy and responsibility of the Federal Government to use all practicable means ... [to create and maintain] conditions which promote useful employment opportunities, including self-employment, for those able, willing, and seeking work, and promote full employment and production."[10]

The bill was originally the "Full Employment Bill," which would have declared Americans had a right to full-time employment. The "right" to a job was removed from the final version because it was viewed as too radical.[11]

When FLSA was legally challenged in the case *United States v. Darby Lumber Co.*, the Supreme Court again overturned its Lochner Era decision. The federal government could now regulate labor conditions.[12]

The Fair Employment Practices Committee of 1941

As the United States stood at the brink of World War II, racial discrimination was still pervasive. Black workers were discriminated against in hiring and wages and were effectively locked out of some industries. New Deal programs such as the National Recovery Administration (created as part of NIRA) routinely promoted discrimination by giving white workers job preference and authorizing a separate—and lower—pay scale for black workers.[13]

A. Philip Randolph founded the Brotherhood of Sleeping Car porters and was a leader in fighting for black labor rights.

A. Philip Randolph, who founded the Brotherhood of Sleeping Car Porters in 1925, was a leader in fighting for black labor rights. On January 25, 1941, he issued a call for a March on Washington to occur on July 1 of that year to protest the continued segregation of the defense industry. By June, organizers were estimating more than 100,000 people would turn out to march in the intensely racially segregated capital. Intimidated and shamed, President Roosevelt offered to sign an executive order forbidding racial discrimination in employment if Randolph would agree to cancel the March on Washington. Roosevelt signed Executive Order 8802 on June 25, and the march was indefinitely postponed.[14]

The executive order prohibited ethnic and racial discrimination in the defense industry and created the Fair Employment Practices Committee (FEPC). The FEPC had a tiny budget and no real enforcement power, though it did draw public attention to offending companies. Unions tried to address workplace discrimination as well, cracking down on "hate strikes" in which white workers went on strike to protest their black counterparts being promoted to "white" positions.

In 1943, Roosevelt tried to strengthen the FEPC with increased funding and staff. His successor, Harry Truman, tried to establish the FEPC as a permanent body, but his efforts were repeatedly stopped by white Southern Democrats. The FEPC ended in 1946. In its five-year span, it oversaw black workers going from 3 percent to 8 percent of the defense industry and 200,000 black people being employed in the federal government, though most of the jobs were low-wage, menial positions. While it was a small step, it was still a first victory for Randolph's movement and an acknowledgment that racial discrimination in employment was a national problem.[15]

CHAPTER
4

Labor Laws of the Civil Rights Era

Massive changes were afoot as World War II ended. Hundreds of thousands of veterans returned to workplaces to find that their jobs had been filled by white women or people of color in their absence. With unions no longer hampered by promises not to interfere with the war effort, strikes wracked the country—4,600 in just twelve months, ranging from fledgling unions demanding recognition to established unions fighting to raise wages in companies that had profited immensely during the war. Striking machinists were attacked by police in January 1946, causing unions to rally under the slogan, "We Will Not Go Back to the Old Days."

However, the "old days" were largely gone. Most of the strikes remained peaceful, and company and government interventions occurred far more often in courts than in violent confrontations on picket lines. The National Labor Relations Act of 1935 had ensured that unions had an enforceable right to organize and bargain, and this discouraged violence from workers as well. By September 1946, more than 5 million workers had been involved in strikes, and business leaders took their case to Congress.[1]

Shown here are workers on strike in 1948, protesting the actions of the owner of a company. On their signs, he is shown basking on a beach, having grown rich from their labor.

The Taft-Hartley Act of 1947

With the end of World War II also came the end of the tentative, somewhat strained alliance between the United States and the Soviet Union, and suspicion of communist influence in

America began to rise with the Cold War. In 1947, President Truman signed Executive Order 9835, demanding that federal employees be screened for "loyalty"; they could not be members of organizations that were "totalitarian, Fascist, Communist or subversive."[2] This marked the beginning of the Second Red Scare in the United States. As the federal government tied itself in knots searching for secretly "disloyal" employees, it created the House Un-American Activities Committee, which spread the hunt for communists out into the public. Witnesses who refused to cooperate were often effectively blacklisted, meaning no one would work with them.[3]

During the Second Red Scare, unions were in the crosshairs of the communist hunters. Anarchists and socialists had been involved in the labor movement since its early days. Anarchists had been found responsible and hanged for the Haymarket Riot in 1886. Socialists such as Lucy Parsons were the founders of the Industrial Workers of the World (IWW) in 1905. After the Bolshevik Revolution of 1917 in Russia, paranoia had raged in America that a similar revolution would come, touching off the First Red Scare. The IWW, with its known socialist roots, had been an easy target, as had been unions in general, with their immigrant-heavy memberships. During the First Red Scare, 3,500 people had been jailed and 556 had been deported on suspicion of being communists or leftists.[4]

With the Second Red Scare dawning in 1947, Congress passed the Taft-Hartley Act. One of its provisions required that all union leaders file affidavits with the Department of Labor to prove they were not members of "subversive" organizations if they wanted to use the NLRB. Other provisions severely limited the gains labor had made with the NLRA, restricting unions and giving companies more power to interfere with their formation. States were given the ability to pass "right-to-work" laws, which meant workers could be fired at any time. Worse, the Taft-Hartley Act caused a major split in the labor movement, with unions who were sympathetic to communists—or at least not interested in participating in the coming witch hunt—being expelled from larger organizations such as the Congress of Industrial Organizations.[5]

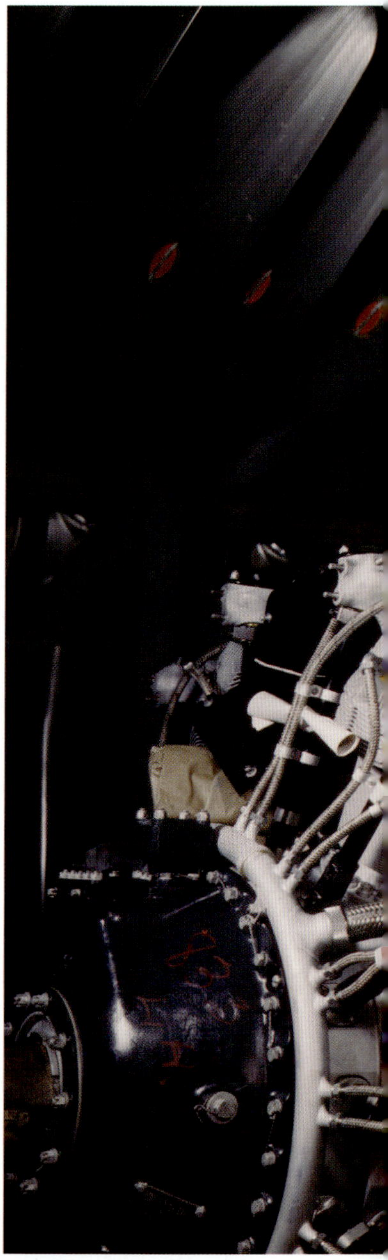

The Equal Pay Act of 1963

During World War II, women streamed into the workforce to take up jobs vacated by male soldiers. At its height, there were more than 19 million women employed during the war, making up 37 percent of the workforce. After the war ended, the majority of women wanted to keep their jobs.[6] While women had been historically paid less than men, the National War Labor Board encouraged employers to pay female workers as much as male workers. The policy wasn't enough to close the pay gap, though; in 1945, the Women's Equal Pay Act was introduced into Congress, but it did not pass.

After the war, women were often forced out of their jobs to make room for returning soldiers. For those who remained, the pay was unequal. Other attempts were made by Congress to address the pay gap during the 1950s, but with no success. By 1960, women were earning less than two-thirds of what men doing the same jobs were paid, despite the large number of women companies employed.

With men away and fighting, women filled the workplace during World War II. They were often forced out of their jobs when men returned home.

In 1961, President John F. Kennedy appointed a labor activist named Esther Peterson to be the head of the Department of Labor's Women's Bureau. At her urging, he established a Presidential Commission on the Status of Women, which Peterson used to gather data and build political will for an equal pay law. She submitted a draft of the bill to Congress in 1963. It was signed into law on June 10, 1963, and became an amendment to FLSA. The new Equal Pay Act demanded that women be paid equally for performing "equal work."[7]

Even today, women are paid less than men for doing equal work. The Equal Pay Act was not a magical cure, but it said that wage discrimination could no longer be embedded in the law and offered women workers a path forward to fight for the wages that were rightfully theirs.

The Civil Rights Act of 1964

While the Fourteenth Amendment supposedly guaranteed all citizens of the United States "equal protection of the laws," racial segregation was a reality across the United States. In some places it was technically illegal but practied anyway, but it was the law in Southern states during the Jim Crow era. This was not something people of color accepted quietly; racist laws had been fought in the courts and protested in the streets since the end of the post–Civil War Reconstruction Era. By the 1950s, a coordinated civil rights movement was organized against racial segregation in all forms.[8]

Under pressure from protests, President Kennedy proposed sweeping civil rights legislation in June 1963, saying that America "will not be fully free until all of its citizens are free."

President John F. Kennedy (*seated*) signs the Equal Pay Act into law, with Esther Peterson (*far left*) attending the occasion.

After Kennedy's assassination five months later, President Lyndon B. Johnson continued the work. Despite attempts by segregationists in Congress to sabotage the bill, Johnson signed the Civil Rights Act into law on July 2, 1964.[9]

The Civil Rights Act (CRA) made big changes, banning segregation in public places. Title VII of the act banned discrimination by employers on the basis of race, religion, national origin, or gender. The CRA also created the Equal

Employment Opportunity Commission (EEOC), an independent regulatory body with the power to sue employers who discriminate against current workers and in hiring practices.

Three years after the Civil Rights Act passed, Congress added the Age Discrimination in Employment Act after it found there was discrimination against older workers as well. This law protected people between the ages of 40 and 70. An amendment in 1986 removed the upper age limit.[10]

With unions weakened and in decline thanks to the Taft-Hartley Act, the various laws protecting workers from discrimination by employers were perhaps intended to pick up

The Pregnancy Discrimination Act of 1978

In 1973, Martha Gilbert joined other female employees of General Electric Company in a class-action lawsuit. They all had insurance from their employer, which included disability benefits for a wide range of sickness and accidents that could happen outside the job. However, any disabilities related to pregnancy, childbirth, or miscarriages were not included. The case went to the Supreme Court in 1976, which decided 6–3 that the exclusion of pregnancy-related disabilities was not actually an indication of sex discrimination because the plan was worth the same amount to both men and women.[11]

As a direct response to *Gilbert v. General Electric Company*, Congress passed the Pregnancy Discrimination Act of 1978, an amendment to the Civil Rights Act of 1964 that prevented sex discrimination "on the basis of pregnancy, childbirth, or related medical conditions."[12]

Continuing the work of Kennedy, Lyndon B. Johnson signed the Civil Rights Act into law with Martin Luther King Jr. at his side.

some of the slack and render unions even less necessary. The burden of action against unfairness in the workplace was left to the individual to bring to the EEOC—but unlike in the decades before the NLRB, there was a government agency on the side of workers.

Modern Labor Laws

The end of the Vietnam War heralded an era of more conservative government. People were suspicious of the military adventurism that had caused America to involve itself in wars in Southeast Asia for nearly twenty years. There was also social pushback against the civil rights gains made by minorities and white women since the end of World War II. The Republican Party gained more power in the federal government, culminating in the election of Ronald Reagan in 1980.

President Reagan led a government that was extremely hostile to unions and friendly to businesses that were still angry about the New Deal reforms that had helped workers. In the first year of his presidency, Reagan effectively broke the back of the Professional Air Traffic Controllers Organization. After 15,000 air traffic controllers walked off the job on August 3, 1981, to protest lack of staffing and modernization that was placing too much strain on people in an already stressful

In 1981, 15,000 air traffic controllers walked off the job to protest a lack of staffing and modernization. Reagan said most strikers who did not return to work would be fired, and he followed through with this threat.

job, Reagan said on national television that any air traffic controllers who did not return to work within two days would be fired. Most were.[1]

Union membership had already begun to drop during the Second Red Scare, but a combination of President Reagan's policies and technological advancements that replaced workers in traditionally union jobs hastened the decline. Union membership dropped from nearly 25 percent in 1980 to about 17 percent in 1988.[2] As of 2018, union membership sat at about 10.5 percent of all workers in the United States, according to the Bureau of Labor Statistics; 33.9 percent of public sector workers were in unions, as opposed to only 6.4 percent in the private sector.[3]

While there has generally been an erosion of labor gains, three new federal laws promised progress and protection for workers.

The Occupational Safety and Health Act of 1970

Workplace safety has long been a major issue for workers. Throughout the Industrial Revolution, workers were regularly harmed by factory machinery and in other industrial accidents. On March 25, 1911, the Triangle Shirtwaist Factory in New York City went up in flames after a small fire started in a bin full of rags. Fire buckets throughout the factory had been allowed to stand empty, and the fire hose on the floor was rotted, its nozzle rusted shut.

The workers, mostly women who operated the sewing machines on the eighth and ninth floors, panicked and tried to flee the building. The fire escape, poorly maintained, collapsed. Doors to the outside were either locked (according to witnesses, something done to prevent theft) or were meant to be pulled open and were kept pressed closed by the crush of panicking workers. People leaped to their deaths from the windows or down the elevator shaft to try to escape the fire. The New York Fire Department, when their trucks began to arrive, didn't have a ladder long enough to reach the floors where the fire was. In just eighteen minutes, 146 people died.

The Triangle Shirtwaist Factory fire killed 146 people because they were unable to escape the building as it burned. In workplace safety protests, these factory workers are still remembered.

In the wake of the horror and union anger at the Triangle Shirtwaist Factory fire, New York State adopted new fire safety measures and labor codes to ensure such an accident could never happen again. These laws became a model for other states, and even later for the New Deal.[4]

Nearly sixty years later, workplace safety came back into the consciousness of the country due to the rising number and severity of industrial accidents. Between 1960 and 1970, 14,000 workers died each year from industrial accidents. In 1967, news broke that almost 100 uranium miners had died of lung cancer since the 1940s, a disproportionately large number that pointed at working conditions as the cause.[5] After false starts on a bill aimed at on-the-job safety during the Johnson administration, the Occupational Safety and Health Act was signed into law by President Richard Nixon on December 29, 1970.

The act established three new agencies; the one many people are most familiar with is the Occupational Safety and Health Administration (OSHA), which works under the Department of Labor. As soon as OSHA was staffed, it began setting industry standards to protect the health of employees. Its first act was to regulate asbestos exposure. Asbestos is a set of fibrous minerals used in heat-resistant products; breathing in microscopic asbestos fibers can cause a variety of cancers and other lung diseases. OSHA has since expanded its standards to a wide variety of toxic and dangerous substances that workers might be exposed to during their jobs, as well as standardizing safety equipment and best practices for industries.

Americans With Disabilities Act of 1990

Throught America's history, people with disabilities have been regularly excluded from public life and discriminated against, even as a matter of law. During the civil rights era, people with disabilities began organizing along

In 1990, George H. W. Bush signed the Americans with Disabilities Act into law, ensuring workplace protections for people with disabilities.

with other groups, fighting for recognition of their own right to exist in public life. Disabled activists had a major victory in 1973, when discrimination against people on the basis of disability was banned for any organization that received federal funding.[6]

Activists continued the fight using lawsuits and direct actions. For example, in 1978, a group of disabled activists blocked an intersection in Denver, Colorado, for an entire day, chanting "We will ride!" in protest of the lack of accessible buses.[7] Groups and individuals worked tirelessly to gather evidence that proved the need for broad anti-discrimination protections to be codified into law. The Americans with Disabilities Act (ADA) rose out of these decades of hard work. It was introduced in 1988 and signed into law on July 26, 1990 by President George H. W. Bush.

The ADA included specific protections for disabled workers, such as specifying that employers could not discriminate in hiring, promotion, firing, pay, or other areas against qualified individuals with disabilities. The ADA also required employers to provide "reasonable accommodations" to workers with disabilities, such as providing special equipment that would allow them to do their job—as long as it's not significantly expensive.[8] One example of "special equipment" would be providing a screen-reading program for a blind or visually impaired worker who deals with computers. Workers can report violations of the ADA to the EEOC.

Family and Medical Leave Act of 1993

One area not protected by the Civil Rights Act or ADA was if someone had to take an extended leave of absence from a job. There are many reasons this could happen: parents want to spend time with new babies; pregnancy, accidents, and serious illnesses can require that someone be out of work longer than

Shown here is President Bill Clinton signing the Family and Medical Leave Act into law. The act ensures that people will not lose their jobs if they have to take time off for family or medical reasons.

they have vacation and sick time to cover; people must take care of sick relatives or children for long periods of time. Until recently, such extended absences often led to workers losing their jobs unless they could negotiate an extended leave with their employer.[9] Individual negotiation of that sort is commonly unfair to workers.

When President Bill Clinton was elected, this problem was one he focused on resolving. His solution was the Family and Medical Leave Act (FMLA), which he signed into law on

February 5, 1993. FMLA allows employees to take up to twelve weeks of unpaid leave in a year for medical or defined family reasons. It guarantees that after the leave is done, the employee has the right to come back to either their same job or one that's comparable in pay and benefits.[10]

While FMLA was a big step forward for Americans, the vast majority of countries in the world have laws that provide for six months or more of paid medical leave.[11]

Right-to-Work Laws

Prompted by the Taft-Hartley Act of 1947, "right-to-work" laws proliferated in the states. These laws state that people cannot be required to join unions; there cannot be "closed shops" that only allow the hiring of union workers. While workers who are not union members still benefit from contracts negotiated by unions, these laws can also interfere with the ability of unions

At-Will vs. Right-to-Work

"Right-to-work" can be easy to confuse with another common term, "at-will." While right-to-work is aimed squarely at who is and is not part of a union, at-will laws effect all employees. At-will employment means that a worker can be fired by an employer at any time, for any *legal* reason—so employees still can't be fired for being part of a protected class.[12]

At-will laws are much older than right-to-work laws. "At-will" started as part of common law that employers just followed by tradition. In the late nineteenth century, workers started to bring legal challenges against the practice. Ultimately, most states enshrined the precedent into law. The only US state without an at-will employment law is Montana.

to collect dues from nonmembers for this service, making these workers what are called "free riders." While these may seem like small things, they can be used to starve unions of funding and membership; people tend not to want to pay to join a union when they can have the benefits for free, but without funding from member dues, unions can't survive, which takes the benefits away from everyone.[13] In recent years, these laws have not been accepted quietly. In 2015, Wisconsin was wracked by massive protests when its legislature passed a right-to-work law.[14] As of 2019, twenty-seven states have these kinds of laws.

Despite right-to-work and other laws that make strikes illegal, teachers' unions turned out across America in 2018 and 2019 to protest low pay and large class sizes in the "Red for Ed" movement. Of the nine cities and states where teachers protested—Arizona, Colorado, Georgia, Kentucky, North Carolina, Oklahoma, Virginia, West Virginia, and Los Angeles (the second-largest public school district in the country)—all but three were successful.[15] In 2018, voters in Missouri rejected a right-to-work law for that state—a surprise to anyone who assumed a traditionally Republican state would be happy to continue the erosion of labor rights.[16] After the 2018 election resulted in Democratic Party gains in state and national legislatures, bills were introduced in Michigan and Virginia to repeal those states' right-to-work laws.[17]

Workers have always fought to have their unions recognized, and the battle continues. The teacher strikes of 2018 and 2019 have shown that anti-labor laws will not stop workers from protesting, just like a lack of unions did not stop workers from taking collective action during the Great Depression.

CHAPTER
6

What Does the Future Hold for American Workers?

Generally, when the United States is compared to the other "advanced economies" of the world, the playing field is more tilted to favor businesses over workers. For example, America is the only "advanced economy" in the world that doesn't actually require employees to receive paid vacation time, making paid vacation in the United States a privilege, not a right.[1] The International Trade Union Confederation rates the United States a 4 on its Global Rights Index, indicating that it has "systematic violations of [workers'] rights."[2]

American workers have had to fight to better their condition since the birth of the country; it's a battle that never ends. History has shown that no victories are permanent—and no losses are, either. What might the future hold for labor laws in the United States?

The Fight for $15

As of 2019, the federally mandated minimum wage is $7.25 and has been for over a decade. Only twenty-nine states have a higher minimum wage. It should also be noted that workers who receive tips, such as waiters, have a much lower minimum wage. The federal minimum wage has not kept pace with inflation, meaning workers are effectively being paid less at the minimum wage than they were in the past.[3] Globally, America

Even today, protests for a higher standard minimum wage across the country continue. Workers who are paid tips generally receive a lower hourly wage.

lags badly in comparison to the rest of the world; the *Economist* noted in 2015 that, taking into account the amount of the US gross domestic product (GDP), American workers should receive a minimum wage of $12 per hour.[4]

While defenders of the low minimum wage like to characterize workers who receive it as young people who don't have many bills and therefore don't need a lot of money, less than half of the people who earn minimum wage are under the age of twenty-four. Even people who work minimum-wage jobs in states or cities where it's higher than the federal wage still don't make what's called a "living wage"—a wage that allows them to pay for food, shelter, and other necessities without requiring public assistance. In 2013, a study showed that 52 percent of fast-food workers made so little that they had to receive public assistance, and 25 percent of the general workforce needed assistance.[5]

In 2012, fast-food workers in New York City went on strike, demanding higher wages and union recognition.[6] More strikes by fast-food workers, many of whom were only paid minimum wage, followed. In 2013, these strikes coalesced into a movement that demanded the minimum wage across the country be raised to $15, which became called "Fight for $15." Since then, four states and several cities have begun to gradually raise their minimum wages to $15.[7] The "Fight for $15" has become increasingly mainstream, with Democratic politicians such as Rashida Tlaib and Gretchen Whitmer promoting the idea in their platforms.[8]

The "Fight for $15" may be best viewed as a first step toward closing the wealth gap in America, which now may actually be worse than it was during the Gilded Age.[9] However, even $15 an hour may not be enough to allow workers to live in most states.

In 2018, hundreds of people occupied congressional offices, protesting for a Green New Deal.

The Green New Deal

In 2018, the Intergovernmental Panel on Climate Change (IPCC) warned that the world had less than twelve years to make radical changes to prevent the worst of the projected climate catastrophes.[10] Despite these dire predictions, politicians in both major US political parties have been slow to offer solutions—and many politicians, particularly members of the Republican Party, deny that climate change even exists.

Activists have offered their own solutions since as early as 2007—a "Green New Deal" that would address both climate change and modern labor issues. There are few details of

Representative Alexandria Ocasio-Cortez pushed for a committee on the Green New Deal and gained the support of many of her fellow representatives and senators.

what the Green New Deal would involve, but the general idea seems to be massive, government-directed investments into changing infrastructure and industry in the country to be environmentally friendly, sustainable, and carbon neutral. This would create a lot of jobs during the shift from a fossil fuel-centered energy economy to a carbon-neutral one.

The idea has become more mainstream and gained national recognition since the 2018 election, with newly-elected representative Alexandria Ocasio-Cortez pushing for a Select Committee on the Green New Deal in Congress and gaining the support of thirty-nine other representatives and senators. The fight for the committee in 2019 was ultimately unsuccessful, but it raised the profile of the proposal and got more people to discuss concrete policy steps and laws.[11]

If the Green New Deal idea gets off the ground and touches on a massive expansion of workers' rights, it could be the new frontier of labor law.

Universal Basic Income

In the past, automation hasn't necessarily made the number of jobs shrink; it's just shifted them from one industry to another. Workers lost jobs in factories as manufacturing machinery became more sophisticated, while more and more jobs opened up in the growing technology industries. That may be how it will always work, but it's worth considering what happens to

Self-Driving Vehicles

In 2018, Google was the first company to be allowed to test self-driving cars on public roads.[12] While the prospect of being able to sit in a car that drives itself while you watch videos might sound great, there are major concerns about the effects the technology could have on workers.

A 2018 report indicated that 4 million jobs are likely to be directly lost due to self-driving vehicles, mostly affecting people who drive trucks or taxis. Truck driving is one of the few industries where workers without a college education are guaranteed a living wage, as the median salary for truck drivers is $42,580 per year. While technology companies working on autonomous vehicles are rapidly hiring workers, truck drivers and software engineers have extremely different skill sets.[13]

In his 2020 presidential campaign, Andrew Yang proposed universal basic income as part of his platform. He called for giving every American over eighteen $1,000 every month.

people who get left behind by the shift in technology—and what happens if the day arrives when there really aren't enough jobs because machines are doing all of the menial work. In 2013, two researchers at Oxford University concluded that over the next two decades, 47 percent of jobs in America could be taken over by machines.[14]

Universal basic income (UBI) is the idea that every person should be provided a set stipend from the government. People would be able to spend that money however they like, and it would be enough to provide them a decent standard of living, which could then be supplemented by wages from a job if a person chooses. UBI has been of particular interest to tech billionaires such as Elon Musk and Mark Zuckerberg, who believe automation may make it a necessity.[15]

One of the oldest UBI trials, which occurred in a small town in Manitoba, Canada, between 1974 and 1978, was called Mincome. During the time it ran, the people in the town showed improved mental health, fewer hospitalizations, and more schooling completed. Counter to fears about basic income, the employment rate didn't change. The Mincome results weren't analyzed until later due to a lack of funding, but they were interesting enough to prompt trials in multiple other countries, including Finland and Kenya.[16] Several pilot programs were cut short in 2018 due to the local governments changing over from liberal to conservative control.[17]

Will UBI become the future of labor, working with automation to provide a sort of utopia where people don't have to work in order to survive? Will there be guaranteed green jobs instead, focused on making local communities better and more accessible for everyone? Perhaps most likely, the future will hold things no one has yet imagined, and the laws will play catch-up as American workers continue the fight for a decent life and a fair share of the profits they produce.

CHRONOLOGY

1790 The Industrial Revolution begins, drawing people into the cities for factory work.

1834 The Lowell mill girls start their first strike to protest pay cuts and bad working conditions.

1861 The American Civil War begins with the attack on Fort Sumter on April 12.

1863 President Abraham Lincoln signs the Emancipation Proclamation and frees all the enslaved people in the South.

1865 The American Civil War ends on April 9, and the Thirteenth Amendment to the Constitution is ratified by the required number of states on December 6.

1870 The Gilded Age begins. It lasts until about 1900.

1873 An economic depression starts in the United States, kicked off by a financial crisis called the Panic of 1873.

1886 The Haymarket Riot occurs on May 4 when, after days of labor protests, an anarchist throws a bomb at armed Chicago police threatening a peaceful gathering. The police fire into the crowd, killing multiple people.

1894 The Pullman Strike paralyzes American railways from June to July until the government violently brings it to an end.

1895 The Supreme Court rejects the government's ability to regulate working conditions in *Lochner v. New York*, signaling the start of the Lochner Era of the court.

1911 The Triangle Shirtwaist Fire kills 146 people in just eighteen minutes on March 25 due to negligence and unsafe working conditions.

1914 The First World War begins on July 28, though the United States does not enter the war until April 6, 1917.

1917 The First Red Scare begins, leading to the persecution of people accused of communism or anarchism. It lasts until 1921.

1929 The Great Depression begins with the stock market crash on October 29 and continues until 1939.

1933 The National Industrial Recovery Act is signed by President Franklin Roosevelt. It suspends antitrust laws and includes massive work conditions improvements. It's declared unconstitutional two years later.

1935 The Social Security Act is passed, in part guaranteeing unemployment insurance for workers who have lost their jobs.

1937 The Supreme Court upholds the minimum wage in *West Coast Hotel Co. v. Parrish*, indicating the end of the Lochner Era.

1938 The Fair Labor Standards Act is passed, ending child labor and guaranteeing a minimum wage.

1939 World War II begins on September 1, though the United States does not formally enter the war until after the attack on Pearl Harbor on December 7, 1941.

1941 The Fair Employment Practices Commission is founded on June 25 after A. Philip Randolph threatens to lead 100,000 people in a March on Washington to protest industrial segregation.

1945 World War II ends on September 2; returning soldiers soon begin taking their jobs back from the women who occupied them during the war.

1947 At the beginning of the Second Red Scare, the Taft-Hartley Act is passed and anti-union right-to-work laws begin to spread across the United States.

1948 President Harry S. Truman issues Executive Order 9981 to end discrimination and segregation in the military.

1963 On August 28, a 200,000-person March on Washington occurs to protest racial discrimination.

1964 President Lyndon Johnson signs the Civil Rights Act. It includes provisions to combat workplace discrimination.

1981 Ronald Reagan breaks a strike by air traffic controllers.

1990 George H. W. Bush signs the Americans with Disabilities Act.

1993 Bill Clinton signs the Family and Medical Leave Act.

2012 Michigan passes a right-to-work law despite large protests by unions in the state.

2018 The "Red for Ed" teacher strikes begin to spread across the United States, even in states where strikes are illegal.

2019 Representative Alexandria Ocasio-Cortez of New York and Senator Edward J. Markey of Massachusetts propose the Green New Deal, which would tackle climate change with sweeping changes to US industries.

Introduction

1. "Equal Pay Activist Lilly Ledbetter Wants to Meet with Ivanka Trump," *CNN Money*, April 10, 2018, money.cnn.com/2018/04/10/pf/lilly-ledbetter-equal-pay-day/index.html.
2. "Equal Payback for Lilly Ledbetter," *Forbes*, April 28, 2009, www.forbes.com/2009/04/28/equal-pay-discrimination-forbes-woman-leadership-wages.html#744c7edc6065.
3. "Ginsburg Dissent: Ledbetter v. Goodyear Tire & Rubber Co. Case Summary," UH School of Law Library, library.law.hawaii.edu/2017/02/02/ledbetter/.
4. "Discrimination by Type," US Equal Employment Opportunity Commission, www.eeoc.gov/laws/types/index.cfm (accessed March 22, 2019).
5. "Discrimination by Type," US Equal Employment Opportunity Commission,
6. Deborah L. Brake and Joanna L. Grossman, "Title VII's Protection Against Pay Discrimination: The Impact of Ledbetter v. Goodyear Tire & Rubber Co.," *Regional Labor Review*, vol. 10 no. 1, Center for the Study of Labor and Democracy, Hofstra University.
7. Brake and Grossman, "Title VII's Protection Against Pay Discrimination: The Impact of Ledbetter v. Goodyear Tire & Rubber Co."
8. "Reading a Dissent from the Supreme Court Bench," National Constitution Center, July 18, 2014, constitutioncenter.org/blog/reading-a-dissent-from-the-supreme-court-bench.
9. "Lilly Ledbetter: RBG's Dissent in Landmark Case Still Gives Me 'Chills,'" CNN, August 22, 2018, www.cnn.com/2018/08/22/politics/rbg-podcast-lilly-ledbetter-cnntv/index.html.
10. "Fact Sheet: New Steps to Advance Equal Pay on the Seventh Anniversary of the Lilly Ledbetter Fair Pay Act," The White

House Office of the Press Secretary, January 29, 2016, obamawhitehouse.archives.gov/the-press-office/2016/01/29/fact-sheet-new-steps-advance-equal-pay-seventh-anniversary-lilly.

11. "Racial, Gender Wage Gaps Persist in U.S. Despite Some Progress," Pew Research Center, July 1, 2016, www.pewresearch.org/fact-tank/2016/07/01/racial-gender-wage-gaps-persist-in-u-s-despite-some-progress/.
12. "The Narrowing, but Persistent, Gender Gap in Pay," Pew Research Center, April 9, 2018, www.pewresearch.org/fact-tank/2018/04/09/gender-pay-gap-facts/.

CHAPTER 1: Labor vs. Monopolies

1. "Rise of Industrial America, 1876–1900," Library of Congress, accessed on August 12, 2019, www.loc.gov/teachers/classroommaterials/presentationsandactivities/presentations/timeline/riseind/.
2. "The Industrial Revolution in the United States," Library of Congress, accessed on August 12, 2019, www.loc.gov/teachers/classroommaterials/primarysourcesets/industrial-revolution/pdf/teacher_guide.pdf.
3. "Lowell Mill Women Create the First Union of Working Women," AFL-CIO, accessed on August 12, 2019, aflcio.org/about/history/labor-history-events/lowell-mill-women-form-union.
4. S. Mintz and S. McNeil, "The Movement for a Ten-Hour Day," *Digital History*, accessed on August 12, 2019, www.digitalhistory.uh.edu/disp_textbook.cfm?smtID=2&psid=3520.
5. "How the History of Slavery in America Offers an Important Labor Day Lesson," *Time*, August 30, 2018, time.com/5377803/slavery-labor-day.
6. "1860 Census: Population of the United States," United States Census Bureau, accessed on August 12, 2019, www.census.gov/library/publications/1864/dec/1860a.html.

7. Lea S. VanderVelde, "The Labor Vision of the Thirteenth Amendment," *University of Pennsylvania Law Review*, vol. 138:437, 1989.
8. Priscilla Murolo and A. B. Chitty, *From the Folks Who Brought You the Weekend* (New York: The New Press, 2003): pp. 100–136.
9. "Atlanta's Washerwomen Strike," AFL-CIO, accessed on August 12, 2019, aflcio.org/about/history/labor-history-events/atlanta-washerwomen-strike.
10. "African Americans and the American Labor Movement," National Archives, accessed on August 12, 2019, www.archives.gov/publications/prologue/1997/summer/american-labor-movement.html.
11. "American Labor Violence: Its Causes, Character, and Outcome," in *The History of Violence in America: A Report to the National Commission on the Causes and Prevention of Violence*, 1969, www.ditext.com/taft/vio-con.html.
12. "The Great Railroad Strike of 1877," *Encyclopedia Britannica*, accessed on August 12, 2019, www.britannica.com/topic/Great-Railroad-Strike-of-1877.
13. Leifur Magnusson and Marguerite A. Gadsby, "Federal Intervention in Railroad Disputes," *Monthly Labor Review*, vol. 11 no. 1.
14. Gale Ahrens, "Lucy Parsons: Mystery Revolutionist, More Dangerous Than a Thousand Rioters," in *Lucy Parsons: Freedom, Equality, Solidarity* (Chicago: Charles H Kerr, 2004): pp. 1–5.
15. "The Origins of Labor Day," PBS, accessed on August 12, 2019, www.pbs.org/newshour/economy/business-july-dec01-labor_day_9-2.
16. *Loewe v. Lawlor*, 208 U.S. 274 (1908).
17. Harry Shulman, "Labor and the Anti-Trust Laws," *Faculty Scholarship Series*, Paper 4622 (1940), digitalcommons.law.yale.edu/fss_papers/4622

CHAPTER 2: The Lochner Era

1. *Adair v. United States*, 208 U.S. 161 (1908).
2. *Lochner v. New York*, 198 U.S. 45 (1905).
3. *Bunting v. Oregon*, 243 U.S. 426 (1917).
4. "History of Child Labor in the United States—Part 2: The Reform Movement," Bureau of Labor Statistics, accessed on August 12, 2019, www.bls.gov/opub/mlr/2017/article/history-of-child-labor-in-the-united-states-part-2-the-reform-movement.htm.
5. "Keating-Owen Child Labor Act of 1916 (1916)," ourdocuments.gov, accessed on August 12, 2019, www.ourdocuments.gov/doc.php?flash=false&doc=59.
6. *Hammer v. Dagenhart*, 247 U.S. 251 (1918).
7. *United States v. Darby Lumber Co.*, 312 U.S. 100 (1941).
8. "An Act to Establish the Minimum Wage Commission and to Provide for the Determination of Minimum Wages for Women and Minors," Acts, 1912, Chapter 706, archives.lib.state.ma.us/actsResolves/1912/1912acts0706.pdf.
9. *Adkins v. Children's Hospital*, 261 U.S. 525 (1923).
10. *Morehead v. New York*, 298 U.S. 587 (1936).
11. "A Brief History of Workers' Compensation," *Iowa Orthopaedic Journal*, v. 19, 1999.
12. *The Wisconsin Blue Book 1937*, compiled by the Wisconsin Legislative Reference Library, p. 243.
13. "Bombing of The Times in 1910 Set Labor Back a Generation," *Los Angeles Times*, October 3, 2010, articles.latimes.com/2010/oct/03/opinion/la-oe-irwin-bombing-20101003.
14. Thomas G. Andrews, *Killing for Coal* (Cambridge, MA: Harvard University Press, 2010): pp. 1–2, 246–273.
15. *Final Report of the Commission on Industrial Relations Including the Report of Basil M. Manly and the Individual Reports and Statements of the Several Commissioners*, reprinted from Senate Doc. No. 415, 64th Congress (Washington, DC: Washington Government Printing Office, 1916): p. 21.

CHAPTER 3: Labor and the New Deal

1. Murolo and Chitty, *From the Folks Who Brought You the Weekend*, pp. 197–241.
2. "The Great Depression," PBS, accessed on August 12, 2019, www.pbs.org/wgbh/americanexperience/features/dustbowl-great-depression.
3. "Norris-La Guardia Act," *Encyclopedia Britannica*, www.britannica.com/event/Norris-La-Guardia-Act
4. The National Industrial Recovery Act, 48 Stat. 195.
5. *Schechter Poultry Corp. v. United States*, 295 U.S. 195 (1935).
6. National Labor Relations Act, 49 Stat. 449.
7. "Unemployment Insurance Program Description and Legislative History," Social Security Office of Retirment and Disability Policy, accessed on August 12, 2019, www.ssa.gov/policy/docs/statcomps/supplement/2012/unemployment.html.
8. *West Coast Hotel Co. v. Parrish*, 300 U.S. 379.
9. Fair Labor Standards Act, 29 U.S. Code § 203.
10. The Employment Act, Ch. 33, Sec. 2, 60 Stat. 23.
11. "Employment Act of 1946," Federal Reserve History, accessed on August 12, 2019, www.federalreservehistory.org/essays/employment_act_of_1946.
12. *United States v. Darby Lumber Co.*, 312 U.S. 100 (1941).
13. "How Racism Has Shaped Welfare Policy in America Since 1935," Associated Press, August 21, 2016, apnews.com/fbd5d3c83e3243e9b03e46d7cb842eaa.
14. "African Americans Threaten March on Washington, 1941," Global Nonviolent Action Database, accessed on August 12, 2019, nvdatabase.swarthmore.edu/content/african-americans-threaten-march-washington-1941.
15. "Fair Employment Practices Committee," *Encyclopedia Britannica*, accessed on August 12, 2019, www.britannica.com/topic/Fair-Employment-Practices-Committee.

CHAPTER 4: Labor Laws of the Civil Rights Era

1. Murolo and Chitty, *From the Folks Who Brought You the Weekend,* pp. 245–248.
2. "Prelude to McCarthyism: The Making of a Blacklist," National Archives, accessed on August 12, 2019, www.archives.gov/publications/prologue/2006/fall/agloso.html.
3. "House Un-American Activities Committee," Harry S. Truman Presidential Library and Museum, accessed on August 12, 2019, www.trumanlibrary.org/dbq/huac.php.
4. "The IWW and the Red Scare 1917–24," *Journey of Contemporary History*, October 1, 1968.
5. "Post World War II Era: Overview," Georgia State University Library, accessed on August 12, 2019, research.library.gsu.edu/c.php?g=115684&p=752502.
6. "Women & World War II," Metropolitan State University of Denver: Camp Hale, accessed on August 12, 2019, msudenver.edu/camphale/thewomensarmycorps/womenwwii.
7. "Equal Pay Act of 1963," National Park Service, accessed on August 12, 2019, www.nps.gov/articles/equal-pay-act.htm.
8. "Civil Rights Movement," History.com, accessed on August 12, 2019, www.history.com/topics/black-history/civil-rights-movement.
9. "Civil Rights Act of 1964," History.com, accessed on August 12, 2019, www.history.com/topics/black-history/civil-rights-act.
10. "A Study of the Age Discrimination in Employment Act of 1967," American Bar Association, accessed on August 12, 2019, www.americanbar.org/groups/gpsolo/publications/gp_solo/2014/november_december/a_study_the_age_discrimination_employment_act_1967.
11. *Gilbert v. General Electric Company*, 429 U.S. 125 (1976).
12. "What to Expect When You're Expecting (and After the Birth of Your Child) ... at Work," United States Department of Labor,

accessed on August 12, 2019, www.dol.gov/oasam/programs/crc/2011-pregnancy-discrimination.htm.

CHAPTER 5: Modern Labor Laws

1. Murolo and Chitty, *From the Folks Who Brought You the Weekend,* pp. 289–291.
2. "Who Killed American Unions?" *Atlantic*, June 7, 2012, www.theatlantic.com/business/archive/2012/06/who-killed-american-unions/258239/.
3. "Union Members—2018," Bureau of Labor Statistics, News Release, January 18, 2019, www.bls.gov/news.release/pdf/union2.pdf.
4. "Remembering the 1911 Triangle Factory Fire," Cornell University, accessed on August 12, 2019, trianglefire.ilr.cornell.edu/index.html.
5. "The Job Safety Law of 1970: Its Passage Was Perilous," US Department of Labor, accessed on August 12, 2019, www.dol.gov/general/aboutdol/history/osha.
6. "The History of the Americans with Disabilities Act," Disability Rights Education & Defense Fund, accessed on August 12, 2019, dredf.org/about-us/publications/the-history-of-the-ada/.
7. "'We Will Ride!' The Origin of the Disability Rights Movement in Denver," Denver Public Library, accessed on August 12, 2019, history.denverlibrary.org/news/we-will-ride-origin-disability-rights-movement-denver-0.
8. Americans with Disabilities Act of 1989, 104 Stat. 327.
9. "History of FMLA," Labor Law Center, accessed on August 12, 2019, www.laborlawcenter.com/education-center/history-of-fmla.
10. Family and Medical Leave Act of 1993, 107 Stat. 6.
11. "Paid Family Medical Leave in the United States: Good for Families, Good for the Economy," UCLA Newsroom, accessed on August 12, 2019, newsroom.ucla.edu/releases/paid-family-

medical-leave-in-the-united-states:-good-for-families-good-for-the-economy.

12. "The At-Will Presumption and Exceptions to the Rule," National Conference of State Legislatures, accessed on August 12, 2019, www.ncsl.org/research/labor-and-employment/at-will-employment-overview.aspx.
13. "The Right to Work Really Means the Right to Work for Less," *Washington Post*, April 24, 2018, www.washingtonpost.com/news/made-by-history/wp/2018/04/24/the-right-to-work-really-means-the-right-to-work-for-less.
14. "U.S. Appeals Court Upholds Wisconsin 'Right-to-Work' Law," *Reuters*, July 12, 2017, www.reuters.com/article/us-wisconsin-labor-idUSKBN19X34T.
15. "Here's What Teachers Accomplished with Their Protests This Year," CNN, May 29, 2018, www.cnn.com/2018/05/29/us/what-teachers-won-and-lost/index.html; and "The L.A. Teachers' Strike Could Be Just the Beginning for California," *Los Angeles Times*, January 28, 2019, www.latimes.com/politics/la-pol-sac-skelton-lausd-teachers-strike-20190128-story.html.
16. "Unions Notch Win in Deep-Red Missouri with Rejection of Right-to-Work Law," CNN, August 8, 2018, www.cnn.com/2018/08/07/politics/missouri-right-to-work-vote/index.html.
17. "Socialist Manassas-Area Delegate Wants to Repeal Right-to-Work Law," *NBC 4 Washington*, January 19, 2019, www.nbcwashington.com/news/local/Socialist-Manassas-Area-Delegate-Wants-to-Repeal-Right-to-Work-Law-504593632.html; and "Michigan Chamber of Commerce Voices Opposition to Legislation Repealing Michigan's Right-to-Work Law," Michigan Chamber of Commerce, www.prnewswire.com/news-releases/michigan-chamber-of-commerce-voices-opposition-to-legislation-repealing-michigans-right-to-work-law-300777762.html.

CHAPTER 6: What Does the Future Hold for American Workers?

1. "U.S. the Only Advanced Economy That Does Not Require Employers to Provide Paid Vacation Time, Report Says," *Forbes*, August 13, 2013, www.forbes.com/sites/tanyamohn/2013/08/13/paid-time-off-forget-about-it-a-report-looks-at-how-the-u-s-compares-to-other-countries/#5d93bc1c6f65.
2. "New ITUC Global Rights Index—The World's Worst Countries for Workers," International Trade Union Confederation, accessed on August 12, 2019, www.ituc-csi.org/new-ituc-global-rights-index-the.
3. "5 Facts About the Minimum Wage," Pew Research Center, accessed on August 12, 2019, www.pewresearch.org/fact-tank/2017/01/04/5-facts-about-the-minimum-wage/.
4. "Minimum Wages Pay Dirt," *Economist*, May 20, 2015, www.economist.com/graphic-detail/2015/05/20/pay-dirt.
5. "Fast-Food Workers Cost Taxpayers Nearly $7 Billion in Welfare Costs," *Denver Post*, October 15, 2013, www.denverpost.com/2013/10/15/fast-food-workers-cost-taxpayers-nearly-7-billion-in-welfare-costs.
6. "New York's Fast Food Workers Strike. Why Now?" MSNBC, November 29, 2012, www.msnbc.com/the-ed-show/new-yorks-fast-food-workers-strike-why-now.
7. "In New Jersey, the Minimum Wage Is Set to Rise to $15 an Hour," *New York Time*, January 17, 2019, www.nytimes.com/2019/01/17/nyregion/nj-minimum-wage.html.
8. "'Fight for $15' Rallies for Higher Minimum Wage, Right to Unionize," *CBS News*, October 2, 2018, www.cbsnews.com/news/15-an-hour-a-higher-wage-but-hardly-a-living.
9. "A New Gilded Age? Wealth Is More Concentrated Than Ever Before," *Salon*, October 27, 2017, www.salon.com/2017/10/27/a-new-gilded-age-wealth-is-more-concentrated-than-ever-before/.

10. "We Have 12 Years to Limit Climate Change Catastrophe, Warns UN," *Guardian*, October 8, 2018, www.theguardian.com/environment/2018/oct/08/global-warming-must-not-exceed-15c-warns-landmark-un-report.
11. "The Green New Deal, Explained," *Vox*, January 7, 2019, www.vox.com/energy-and-environment/2018/12/21/18144138/green-new-deal-alexandria-ocasio-cortez.
12. "Volvo's Self-Driving Car Venture Gets Nod to Test on Swedish Roads," *Reuters*, January 28, 2019, www.reuters.com/article/us-volvo-autonomous/volvos-self-driving-car-venture-gets-nod-to-test-on-swedish-roads-idUSKCN1PM1J2.
13. "Autonomous Vehicles Won't Only Kill Jobs. They Will Create Them, Too," CNBC, August 11, 2018, www.cnbc.com/2018/08/10/autonomous-vehicles-are-creating-jobs-heres-where.html.
14. "A Study Finds Nearly Half of Jobs Are Vulnerable to Automation," *Economist*, April 24, 2018, www.economist.com/graphic-detail/2018/04/24/a-study-finds-nearly-half-of-jobs-are-vulnerable-to-automation.
15. "Elon Musk: Free Cash Handouts 'Will Be Necessary' if Robots Take Humans' Jobs," CNBC, June 18, 2018, www.cnbc.com/2018/06/18/elon-musk-automated-jobs-could-make-ubi-cash-handouts-necessary.html.
16. "Money for Nothing: The Truth About Universal Basic Income," *Nature*, May 30, 2018, www.nature.com/articles/d41586-018-05259-x.
17. "Universal Basic Income Had a Rough 2018," *MIT Technology Review*, December 27, 2018, www.technologyreview.com/s/612640/universal-basic-income-had-a-rough-2018.

discrimination Unjust treatment or prejudice against people for a characteristic they possess, such as their gender or race.

general strike A strike that is not limited to one union or one industry; a large portion of all workers in a city or region participate.

labor union An organization of workers in a particular trade, profession, or industry that seeks to protect the rights of its members.

minority report A secondary report presented by members of a committee who disagree with the majority to some extent.

monopoly A company that has no serious competitors in its market. It can raise prices counter to market forces and exclude competition.

pervasive Spread widely through a group or area.

proliferate Rapidly increase in number.

regulations Rules adopted by government agencies that enforce laws.

segregation The enforced separation of people, historically by racial group.

socialist A person who believes that the means of production, distribution, and exchange should be owned by the community instead of individuals; an economic theory opposing capitalism.

subsistence farming A type of agriculture where farmers grow crops only to feed themselves and their families rather than to sell to others.

subversive During the Red Scares, someone who wanted to undermine the government of the United States.

sweatshop Shorthand for factory jobs that didn't pay enough for workers to live on while forcing them to work long hours in poor conditions.

working class A social group made up of people who sell their labor for wages. This is historically associated with manual labor, or industrial or factory work. In modern America, the working class is largely made up of people in the service industries.

FURTHER READING

BOOKS

Ashby, Steven K., and Robert Bruno. *A Fight for the Soul of Public Education: The Story of the Chicago Teachers Strike*. Ithaca, NY: Cornell University Press, 2016.

Chang, Grace. *Disposable Domestics: Immigrant Women Workers in the Global Economy*. Chicago, IL: Haymarket Books, 2016.

Moore, Kate. *The Radium Girls*. Naperville, IL: Sourcebooks, Inc, 2016.

Windham, Lane. *Knocking on Labor's Door: Union Organizing in the 1970s and the Roots of a New Economic Divide*. Chapel Hill, NC: The University of North Carolina Press, 2017.

WEBSITES

Disability Rights Education & Defense Fund
dredf.org
This disability rights organization provides information about the Americans with Disabilities Act, its history, and the continued fight for the rights of disabled workers.

The Living Wage Calculator
livingwage.mit.edu
This interactive website features articles about the living wage and a calculator that shows what the living wage might be across America by county.

OurDocuments.gov
www.ourdocuments.gov
This government website stores 100 "milestone" documents in American history and explains them—including labor laws.

Remembering the 1911 Triangle Fire
trianglefire.ilr.cornell.edu
This collection of primary sources and essays examines the Triangle Shirtwaist Factory Fire and its aftermath.

The United States Department of Labor, Bureau of Labor Statistics
www.bls.gov
Information, research papers, and everything related to labor as officially tracked in America can be found on this website.

INDEX